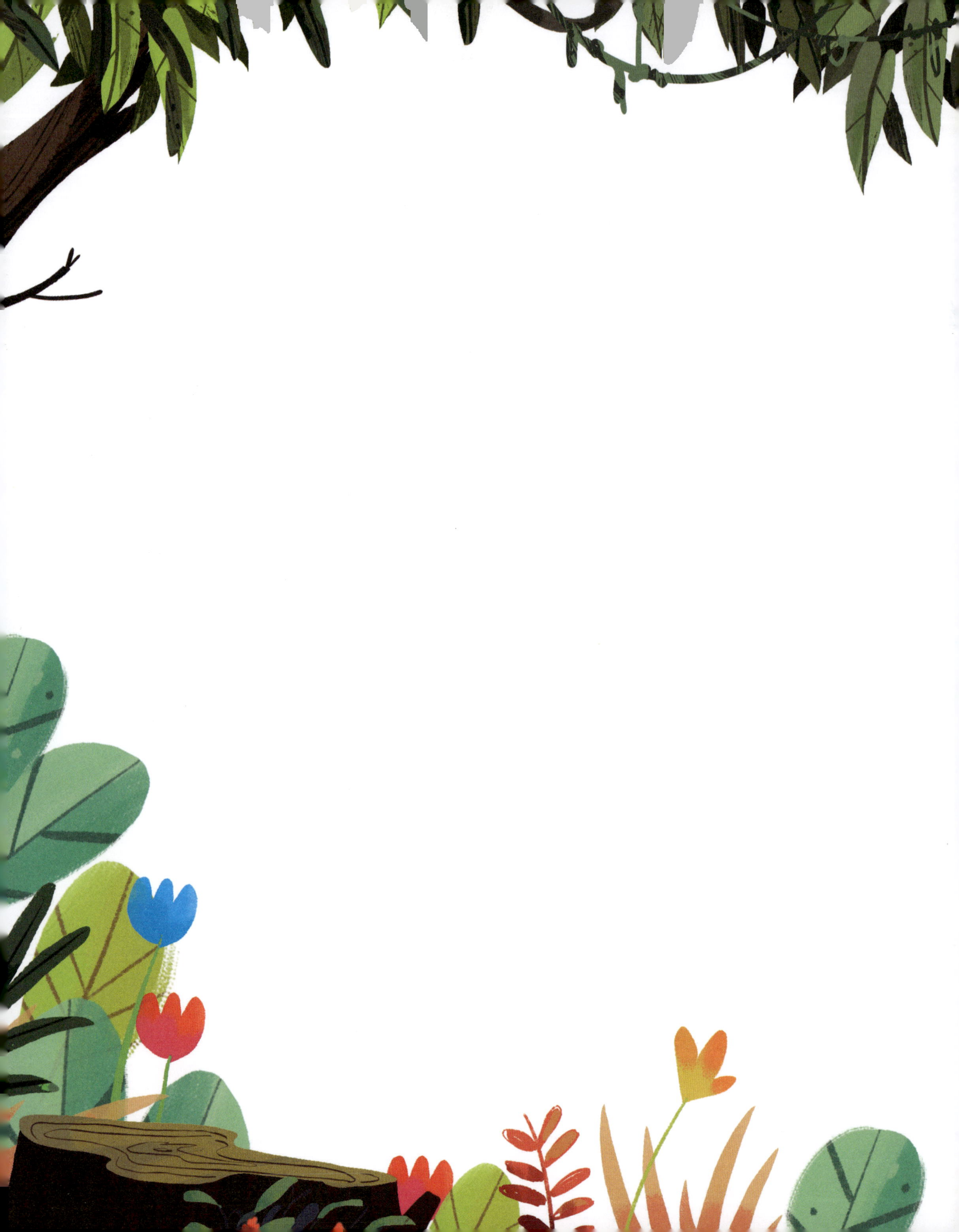

TOGETHER IS BETTER!
Teamwork in the Animal Kingdom

whitestar·kids

CONTENTS

- TEAMWORK IS EVERYWHERE - PAGE 4

- CHIMPANZEE GROOMING - PAGE 6

- PENGUIN HUDDLES - PAGE 8

- WHALES AND BARNACLES - PAGE 10

- BRAVE MEERKATS - PAGE 12

- ZEBRAS AND OSTRICHES - PAGE 14

- "SHEPHERD" ANTS AND 6-LEGGED "SHEEP" - PAGE 16

- FAITHFUL PIGEONS - PAGE 18

- JAPANESE MACAQUE GOURMETS - PAGE 20

- GENEROUS BEE-EATERS - PAGE 22

- CLOWN FISH AND TOXIC ANEMONES - PAGE 24

- THE BEE FORTRESS - PAGE 26

- FRIENDLY SHARKS AND PILOT FISH - PAGE 32

- THE VILLAGE OF SOCIAL SPIDERS - PAGE 34

- GENEROUS VAMPIRES - PAGE 36

- BATTLE-READY BUFFALOES - PAGE 38

- LOVESICK ANUBIS BABOONS - PAGE 40

- SUPPORTIVE RAVENS - PAGE 42

- RATS WITH A HEART OF GOLD - PAGE 44

- DOLPHINS WHO CARE FOR OTHERS - PAGE 46

- VORACIOUS TREE SHREWS AND PLANT TOILETS - PAGE 48

- SELFLESS FIDDLER CRAB - PAGE 50

- THE ABILITY TO COOPERATE IS THE ANSWER - PAGE 52

- MORE TO DISCOVER - PAGE 54

TEAMWORK IS EVERYWHERE

Nature documentaries have shown us plenty of sharp fangs, lethal claws, leaping predators, and terrified prey on the run.

On the screen we have seen deer ramming antlers, birds pecking mercilessly, walruses brutally crushing each other, and wolves knocking down opponents to prove their dominance.

WHAT A MESS!

For years, many thought that nature was just this: an eternal struggle in which every animal looked out just for itself and only the strongest survived. In reality, that is simply...

NOT TRUE!

Across the savannas, jungles, mountain tops, and deep seas, there is another (and very popular) tendency: to collaborate.

WORK TOGETHER, TEAM UP, AND COOPERATE

That's what a lot of animals do, both within their own group and across different species (not to mention the strong collaboration between animals, plants, and mushrooms). The reason is very simple: helping and supporting each other benefits everyone.

LET'S DISCOVER HOW...

CHIMPANZEE GROOMING

SCIENTIFIC NAME: Pan troglodytes

In a team, it is essential to take care of each other.

TEAM SIZE: 10-60 individuals

In groups of chimpanzees, it is very common to see one individual approach another and begin to delouse it, grabbing the parasites with its fingers and tossing them in its mouth. One might think that the chimpanzees are just looking for snacks as they munch on the insects crawling through the fur of their fellow chimps, but that's not the case.

When animals clean each other it is called grooming, and it is an essential part of forming alliances within a group.

A chimpanzee cleans whomever it wants to keep close. It's a way of saying, "I'm your friend. Will you be my friend?"

Cats do it, too, when they lick each other, and so do many other animals, such as parrots, horses, and beavers. That way they know they can cooperate.

IN THIS CATEGORY, CHIMPANZEES ARE PROS!

THEY EAT fruit, seeds, flowers, snails, small bugs.

THEY LIVE in the tropical forests of west-central Africa.

BY TAKING CARE OF EACH OTHER THIS WAY, CHIMPANZEES STRENGTHEN THE BONDS THAT UNITE THEM AND MAKE THEIR TEAM STRONGER EVERY DAY!

WEIGHT: 77-132 lbs (35-60 kg)
HEIGHT: 2.5-4 ft (80-130 cm)

PENGUIN HUDDLES

SCIENTIFIC NAME: Aptenodytes forsteri

Brrrr it's cold! There's only one solution: unity creates heat!

TEAM SIZE: up to thousands of individuals

The South Pole certainly isn't the easiest place to live: temperatures can reach as low as -58°F (-50°C), and the icy wind can blow up to 125 miles (200 km) per hour! In order to stay warm in this frozen land, emperor penguins huddle together and lean against each other, holding their eggs and chicks on their legs. This way the penguins on the outer edge of the circle act like a blanket covering those in the center. It's nice and warm inside!

The temperature in the middle of the group can exceed 85°F (30°C), sometimes reaching almost 105°F (40°C), hotter than a sunny day on the beach. What about the penguins standing on the outside, exposed to the freezing winds? They certainly aren't abandoned.

ON THE CONTRARY, A STEADY ROTATION ENSURES THEY GET A TURN INSIDE THE WARM CENTER.

THEY EAT herring, squid, and krill.

WEIGHT: 44-88 lbs (20-40 kg)
HEIGHT: up to 4 ft (125 cm)

BY SQUEEZING CLOSE TOGETHER, THEY FORM A SHAPE THAT LOOKS ALMOST LIKE A GIANT EGG FROM ABOVE. THIS IS HOW THE WHOLE GROUP SURVIVES THE COLD.

THEY LIVE in Antarctica, around the South Pole.

WHALES AND BARNACLES

SCIENTIFIC NAMES: Balenopetra musculus and Cirripedia

A free ride ... across the oceans.

TEAM SIZE: hundreds of barnacles + 1 whale

The future for a young barnacle is full of possibilities. Newborns roam the ocean as larvae, searching for any surface they can attach to thanks to their adhesive antennae. Some of them bump into a whale, and the slimy skin of this mammal is like winning the lottery. For them, the whale is an excellent means of transportation through the water. The barnacle simply opens its mouth—a bit like a dog sticking its head out of a car window—and food-filled water comes flowing in all on its own. It's an all-day buffet. What about the whales? Do they get any advantage from being carpeted with these little crustaceans? Many scientists believe they do.

THE BARNACLES ACT LIKE STRONG ARMOR TO PROTECT THEIR WHALE AGAINST TERRIBLE ORCA BITES.

THEY LIVE in every ocean in the world.

10

WHALES CAN ALSO USE BARNACLES WHEN FIGHTING FOR A MATE. DURING A BATTLE, THE CRUSTACEANS CAN BECOME TERRIBLY SHARP WEAPONS.

THEY EAT krill.

WEIGHT: about 160 tons
LENGTH: about 33 yards (30 m)

A HUMPBACK WHALE CAN HOST UP TO 990 LB (450 KG) OF BARNACLES

LENGTH: from a quarter-inch (0.5 cm) to 2 in (5 cm)

THEY EAT by filtering plankton suspended in the water.

11

BRAVE MEERKATS

SCIENTIFIC NAME: Suricata suricatta

On the front line to defend the group.

TEAM SIZE: up to 40 individuals

The arid shrublands where meerkats live are extremely dangerous environments for these mongooses. Anyone bigger than them—and most animals are—can eat them in a single bite. That's why, when they emerge from their underground burrows early in the morning in search of food, the meerkats move as a coordinated team.

The hunters search the land for eggs, reptiles, and insects to take back to the colony, while others act as sentries by standing up straight and constantly turning their heads from one side to the other. As soon as they've spotted an enemy, they let out a series of high-pitched barks. It is a precise signal, warning everyone where the danger is and whether the predator is coming from the sky, like a martial eagle, or from the ground, like a jackal.

MANY ANIMAL GROUPS USE SENTRIES THAT SOUND ALARMS. THESE ARE PARTICULARLY BRAVE INDIVIDUALS BECAUSE PREDATORS FOCUS ON THEM WHILE THE OTHERS RUN TO SAFETY.

THEY LIVE in arid habitats of southern Africa.

IT DOESN'T MATTER IF THE SENTRIES ARE OLD EXPERTS OR YOUNG BEGINNERS: EVERYONE TRUSTS THEM.

WEIGHT: less than 2 lbs (1 kg)
HEIGHT: about 12 in (30 cm)

THEY EAT beetles and butterflies, but also small reptiles and scorpions.

ZEBRAS AND OSTRICHES

SCIENTIFIC NAME: Equus quagga and Struthio camelus

A perfect team, in every way.

THEY LIVE in central-southern Africa.

TEAM SIZE: a few dozen zebras and ostriches

Among the zebra herds that slowly graze the African plains with their heads down it is not uncommon to see dozens of ostrich heads popping up nervously to look left and right. The reason is simple enough: ostriches and zebras help each other to protect themselves from predators. They have complementary senses. The ostrich has a poor sense of smell and hearing but excellent vision, thanks to its long neck and large eyes. Meanwhile, the zebra is the opposite. The zebra can't see as well, but it can smell danger, or hear it thanks to long rotating ears, well before ostriches can. By using their senses together they are able to constantly monitor every aspect of their surrounding environment.

BOTH SPECIES HAVE THEIR OWN WAY OF WARNING EACH OTHER TO ESCAPE IF NECESSARY.

Young zebras have brown stripes, and no two patterns are the same! Ostriches are the largest birds in the world and have the largest eyes of any vertebrate on Earth.

THEIR ESCAPING ABILITIES ARE THE SAME: BOTH ZEBRAS AND OSTRICHES CAN REACH 37 MILES (60 KM) PER HOUR.

THEY EAT:
Zebras mostly eat grass. Ostriches also eat grass, as well as seeds, fruits, and flowers.

WEIGHT:
up to 290 lbs (130 kg)
HEIGHT:
over 6.5 ft (2 m)

WEIGHT:
550-705 lbs (250-320 kg)
LENGTH:
6.5-8 ft (2-2.5 m)

"SHEPHERD" ANTS AND 6-LEGGED "SHEEP"

SCIENTIFIC NAME: Lasius niger and Aphis phabae

Supporting each other.

TEAM SIZE: hundreds of individuals

Aphids are tiny plant parasites. These dark little insects feed by piercing plants with their straw-shaped mouths to suck out the sugary sap. They are so greedy that they eat more than they can even hold, forcing them to expel it back out all over the plant. However, it so happens that this substance, called honeydew, is a favorite of black ants. Thus, a sort of pact was born between ants and aphids. Aphids "give" ants the excess honeydew while the ants do their best to protect aphids from their natural predators, such as certain wasps, flies, or fearsome ladybugs that specifically hunt aphids.

It's not unusual to see furious battles between hungry ladybugs and protective ants who have no intention of giving up their flock of aphids without a fight!

THE BLACK ANT ALSO "BABYSITS" FOR SILVER-STUDDED BLUE BUTTERFLIES. IT EXTRACTS AN EDIBLE SWEET SUBSTANCE FROM ITS LARVAE AND PROVIDES PROTECTION IN RETURN.

THEY LIVE across Europe and in many parts of the world.

THE TEAMWORK BETWEEN ANTS AND APHIDS IS LIKE SHEPHERDS PROTECTING THEIR FLOCK OF SHEEP!

WEIGHT: up to 0.0003 oz (10 mg)
LENGTH: 3-5 mm

THEY LIVE throughout the Northern Hemisphere, as well as in Africa and South America.
LENGTH: 2 mm

FAITHFUL PIGEONS

A rock-solid couple!

SCIENTIFIC NAME: Columba livia

TEAM SIZE: 2 birds: a male and a female

Animals that produce hundreds of eggs—such as fish and frogs—don't have to worry if they lose a few. On the other hand, animals that have only a few children, such as mammals, must be vigilant to ensure that all of them survive. Birds also make very few eggs, so they are very careful to nurture them, as well as the resulting chicks. To do this, the mom and dad pigeons work together to make a perfect team. Most of their roles are identical and perfectly interchangeable. Both gather materials for the nest and help build it together. Then they take turns sitting on the eggs and hunting until the chicks hatch. At this point, they both help to feed their young. How they do this is quite extraordinary: they produce a whitish substance, called pigeon milk, that they use to feed their offspring.

BOTH MOM AND DAD FEED THEIR CHILDREN UNTIL THEY GROW UP.

THEY LIVE all over the world.

WEIGHT:
up to 13 oz (380 g)

WINGSPAN:
about 27.5 in (70 cm)

THE RELATIONSHIP BETWEEN PIGEONS LASTS A LIFETIME. A SMALL TEAM, BUT TRULY ROCK SOLID!

THEY EAT
anything, but they especially love grains.

JAPANESE MACAQUE GOURMETS

SCIENTIFIC NAME: Macaca fuscata

Playing together means growing together.

TEAM SIZE: a dozen individuals

Playing is very important for a macaque. When you play, you build trust with your teammates, learn to do activities together, and make plenty of new discoveries as well. One famous example is the discovery of salted potatoes. Here's how it happened: a young macaque who lived on Koshima Island was playing on the beach with a sweet potato she happened to find in the sand. Then the tuber accidentally fell into the salty sea. Discovery: It tasted so much better! All her friends started copying the new game, each discovering how tasty the salted potatoes were. It was a fundamental discovery for the entire population on the island.

THEY LIVE all over Japan, except the north.

WITHIN A SHORT TIME, THE WHOLE MACAQUE COMMUNITY WAS IMITATING THE YOUNGER GENERATION, EATING POTATOES SEASONED BY THE SALTY OCEAN.

WEIGHT:
18-22 lbs (8-10 kg)
LENGTH:
20-22 in (50-55 cm)

THEY EAT
everything, from the bark of plants to insects.

GENEROUS BEE-EATERS

SCIENTIFIC NAME: Merops apiaster

Generations of babysitters that are always available!

TEAM SIZE: from a few dozen to hundreds of individuals

Bee-eaters are colorful birds with blue, green, yellow, black, brown, and orange feathers who all live together near ponds, lakes, and waterways. There they dig into the ground or into sandbanks to build nests for their eggs and chicks. For most birds, the young are usually cared for by their mother and father. But that's not how it works in the world of bee-eaters.

In fact, many of these birds, sometimes almost half of them, decide not to have any children at all. Instead, they devote their entire lives to helping other couples with their offspring. And when there aren't many insects to eat, the number of generous individuals increases still further.

THIS WAY, WHEN FOOD IS SCARCE, THERE ARE FEWER BEAKS TO FEED.

THEY LIVE mostly in southern Europe as well as western and central Asia.

WEIGHT: 1.5-2.5 oz (50-70 g)

WINGSPAN: about 20 in (50 cm)

LENGTH: 10-12 in (25-30 cm)

BEE-EATERS ARE KNOWN AS THE MOST SELFLESS OF BIRDS BECAUSE, INSTEAD OF FOCUSING ON THEIR OWN CHILDREN, THEY CONSIDER THE SURVIVAL OF THE ENTIRE COMMUNITY TO BE MORE IMPORTANT.

THEY EAT
venomous bugs, like bees and hornets. They grab the insects and hit them on a hard surface to remove the stinger and venom.

23

CLOWN FISH AND TOXIC ANEMONES

SCIENTIFIC NAME: Amphiprioninae (family) and Heteractis magnifica

An undersea alliance.

TEAM SIZE: 1 anemone + 5-6 fish

Who would ever want to swim into a tangle of venomous tentacles? This is precisely what clown fish do when they choose to live among sea anemones, incredible animals that look like plants but are actually related to jellyfish. These two types of animals are linked to each other: the anemone needs the clown fish to keep it free of parasites, and the fish hide from predators inside the wavy tentacles of the anemone, safely tucked away in a venomous fortress. They also feed each other: the fish eat the dead tentacles of the anemone and remnants of other fish killed by the venom, while the anemone feeds and grows thanks to waste produced by the fish.

THIS ALLIANCE WAS MADE POSSIBLE BY THE EVOLUTION OF THE CLOWN FISH, MAKING IT IMMUNE TO THE VENOM OF THE ANEMONE.

THEY LIVE in the coral reefs of the Indo-Pacific Oceans and the Red Sea.

SIZE:
A clownfish is small, at 4-6 in (10-15 cm), while anemones can be as large as 1 yd (1 m) in diameter.

MANY KINDS OF ANEMONES TEAM UP WITH OTHER ANIMALS. ONE OF THEM IS EVEN WILLING TO TURN INTO A VENOMOUS BOXING GLOVE FOR ... CRABS!

THE BOXER CRAB USES ANEMONES TO WARD OFF OPPONENTS.

ARCHITECT BEE
Architect bees produce wax and use it to build hexagonal cells, the rooms in which bees store larvae, pollen, and nectar.

THE HIVE IS A COMMUNITY WHERE EVERYONE HAS A JOB.

THE INSIDE OF A HIVE IS DARK, BUT THE BEES ARE ABLE TO ORIENT THEMSELVES PERFECTLY. THEY HAVE DEEP CONVERSATIONS, EVEN IF SILENT. THEY COMMUNICATE WITH SMELLS OR SPECIAL MOVEMENTS AND DANCES. INFORMATION IS EXCHANGED SO THAT EACH BEE UNDERSTANDS WHAT IS NEEDED TO HELP THE ENTIRE HIVE SURVIVE.

CLEANER BEE
Younger bees are the cleaners; they keep the cells free of dirt.

FORAGER BEE
The oldest bees (22-30 days old) are those who go out searching for food. When they come back with their load of food, they put the pollen into pollen cells. The nectar is passed from mouth to mouth, in a long chain of bees that ends in another cell. This one, once full, is sealed with wax. The nectar becomes honey, which is consumed later.

GUARD BEE
Sting venom is produced in bees after they are two weeks old. Once this happens, bees are ready to defend the hive.

THE BEE FORTRESS

SCIENTIFIC NAME: Apis mellifera

THEY LIVE all over the world.

A united team is unbeatable.

TEAM SIZE: tens of thousands of individuals

Bees fly for miles, exploring the land for food. They suck the nectar of flowers, a sugary substance that plants use to attract bees, and also collect flower pollen, which provides energy just like meat or legume proteins do for us. Of course, the foragers often nibble a bit of pollen and suck a little nectar for themselves, but most of the food they collect is destined for the entire hive. The nectar is sucked out using a kind of proboscis and stored in a special bag inside the body. Meanwhile, the pollen ends up all over the bees' hairy bodies. Using their paws as brushes, they diligently pluck it from the hairs and knead it with some nectar to form a ball, which they then attach to bristles on their hind legs. Now they're ready to return to the hive.

LET'S TRY TO FOLLOW ONE!

THEY LIVE mostly in human-made hives. However, they can also nest in natural holes and cavities.

SIZE: A worker bee is 0.5 in (12 mm) long and weighs 0.003 oz (100 mg).

NURSE BEE
Nurse bees feed the larvae. Without them, the little ones would starve.

QUEEN BEE
The queen mates just once in her life with about 8 males. Then she starts laying eggs. All the bees are her children.

DRONE
Male bees are called drones. They try to mate with the queens in other hives. When they aren't doing that, they help the nurse bees feed the small larvae.

FRIENDLY SHARKS AND PILOT FISH

SCIENTIFIC NAME: Naucrates ductor and Carcharhinus longimanus

Big animals helping smaller ones (and vice versa).

TEAM SIZE: 1 shark + a dozen pilot fish

The whitetip shark is a voracious animal. It hunts squid, octopus, tuna, mackerel, and barracuda. However, it doesn't lay a fin on the striped fish that dart around it, following it to every corner of the ocean. That's because these fish, the pilot fish, are indispensable to the shark. They eliminate parasites on the shark's skin and, most importantly, clean its mouth by feeding on the pieces of meat that get stuck between its teeth. They're basically living toothbrushes. This makes the shark and the pilot fish a perfect team. The great predator feeds the fish and protects them from enemies, while the fish keep the shark in perfect health. They are called "pilot" fish because it was once believed that they were piloting the larger animals toward their prey!

THEY LIVE in warm seas all over the world.

THESE FISH ARE ALSO ASSOCIATED WITH RAYS AND SEA TURTLES.

SIZE: They weigh 330 lbs (150 kg). The largest shark ever found of this type was 13 ft (4 m) long.

SIZE:
They're about 2 ft (60 cm) long, and they change color when excited.

THIS KIND OF RELATIONSHIP, WHERE ANIMALS OF DIFFERENT SPECIES HELP EACH OTHER, IS A VERY SPECIAL VERSION OF TEAMWORK CALLED MUTUALISTIC SYMBIOSIS.

THE VILLAGE OF SOCIAL SPIDERS

SCIENTIFIC NAME: Anelosimus studiosus

The benefits of joining a network.

TEAM SIZE: from 50 to a few thousand spiders

Anelosimus spiders are a nightmare for anyone who fears arachnids. They build massive webs from which hang thousands of constantly scurrying spiders. Although the spiders all look the same, or mostly the same, there are actually two types of spiders with opposite personalities: a large number of them are aggressive, while the others are rather docile. Depending on their personality, each spider performs different jobs. The aggressive ones build the web, defend the nest, and capture the insects that get trapped, cutting them up into pieces to feed everyone. The docile ones, on the other hand, are responsible for raising the young. They can be found carefully positioned over spherical clusters containing thousands of eggs.

ONCE THE EGGS HATCH, THE NEW YOUNG SPIDERS ALSO START WORKING FOR THE WHOLE COMMUNITY.

LENGTH: about 8 mm

THE WEB IS LIKE A BIG VILLAGE WHERE EVERYONE HELPS EACH OTHER. THESE HUGE SPIDERWEBS CAPTURE PREY 10 TIMES LARGER THAN WHAT A SINGLE SPIDER CAN CATCH ON ITS OWN.

THEY LIVE in the forests of the Americas.

THEY EAT insects.

GENEROUS VAMPIRES

SCIENTIFIC NAME: Desmodus rotundus

Blood belongs to everyone!

TEAM SIZE: 500-1,000 individuals

Vampire bats have a generous nature; they want everyone, even the most feeble, to be properly fed at all times. They go hunting at night in search of an animal to sink their sharp teeth into, then they make a tiny cut in their victim's skin and lick the drops of blood directly from the wound. First, they satisfy their own hunger, then they fill their mouth with extra blood. Back in the caves where they live with hundreds of other bats, they start giving away the blood they collected in their mouths. They also donate it to other hunter bats, the ones who return still hungry, even if they don't know them. This tradition of food sharing, however, can cause some bats to become very lazy. "Why should I bother hunting," they might ask themselves, "if someone else will feed me?"

HOWEVER, THESE SELFISH BATS DON'T SURVIVE LONG IN VAMPIRE SOCIETY: THE OTHER BATS IMMEDIATELY STOP FEEDING THEM.

ANYONE WHO DOESN'T COOPERATE IS IMMEDIATELY PUT IN THEIR PLACE! IT'S NO JOKE: LEARNING TO WORK AS A GROUP IS ESSENTIAL FOR SURVIVAL!

Zzz

THEY LIVE
in Central and South America, often near herds of cows.

THEY EAT
blood from various animals, especially cows, but also frogs and snakes.

WEIGHT:
1–1.5 oz (30–40 g)

LENGTH:
2.7 to 3.5 in (70–90 mm)

37

BATTLE-READY BUFFALOES

SCIENTIFIC NAME: Syncerus caffer

All united to protect the little ones.

TEAM SIZE: from a few dozen to hundreds of individuals

Lions will often try to eat a small buffalo. Hoping for a chance to attack a calf that has fallen behind, the lion sneaks up on massive herds covering huge portions of the savanna. However, no matter how hard it tries, this is one situation where the "king" rarely succeeds. Buffaloes use their bodies to create a dark, impenetrable barrier that surrounds their young and protects them like a fortress of muscle. As with many animals, it doesn't matter whether the young are related to them or not; African buffaloes protect all the calves in their herd, with no exceptions. If a calf happens to be attacked, the whole herd races to help it without hesitation. The prey comes together in one massive group to turn against the predators, thus reversing their roles.

THE LIONS HAVE NO CHOICE BUT TO RUN IF THEY DON'T WANT TO BE TRAMPLED.

THEY LIVE in the savannas of sub-Saharan Africa.

BUFFALOES OFTEN FIGHT AMONG THEMSELVES, BUT ALL BATTLE CEASES WHEN THE YOUNG ARE IN DANGER.

WEIGHT: up to 1,900 lbs (870 kg)
LENGTH: up to 11.5 ft (3.5 m)

THEY EAT grasses and small shrubs.

LOVESICK ANUBIS BABOONS

SCIENTIFIC NAME: Papio anubis

Teaming up for love.

TEAM SIZE: an unshakable pair

When a male Anubis baboon finds a female, he becomes extremely jealous. He swells his muscles and shows his fangs to any other male who dares to approach or touch his wife. And if the suitor takes it a step too far, the angry baboon attacks violently, chasing him for several yards, hitting, biting, and shoving all the way. The young males who are left as bachelors often end up making a pact: they form an alliance to give each other some alone time with the wife of the dominant male. The agreement is very simple; moving in pairs, one of them sacrifices himself as bait for the older baboon, drawing him away from his wife so that the other is free to flirt with her. Soon after, the two young males switch roles; the one who hasn't yet suffered a beating takes a turn distracting the jealous old baboon, while the battered friend gets his own chance for love with the female of his dreams.

WEIGHT: about 55 lb (25 kg)
LENGTH: up to 3 ft (1 m)

THE TWO YOUNG BABOONS ARE NOT RELATIVES—PROOF THAT ALTRUISM EXISTS EVERYWHERE, NOT JUST WITH FAMILY.

THEY LIVE in the savannas, steppes, and certain forests of central Africa.

THEY EAT everything, from plant roots to chickens.

SUPPORTIVE RAVENS

SCIENTIFIC NAME: Corvus corax

Everyone deserves the same resources.

TEAM SIZE: 50-100 individuals

When a hungry young raven discovers a dead elk in a distant corner of North America's vast spruce forests, it doesn't take a single bite. Instead, it flies around the carcass, memorizing details, then flies off with an empty stomach. A few days later, it returns with about 40 friends. Everyone feasts on the elk and flies away later in the evening. Each of them spreads word of the delicacy they discovered in the forest, and within a week more than 100 ravens have had their turn to eat. We might assume that such a precious supply of food should be defended by sharp beaks and claws, and certainly never shared. On the contrary, food sharing actually works very well. Ravens know that you can't do it alone.

THEY LIVE in North America.

THIS GENIUS IDEA IS ONLY FOUND AMONG YOUNGER RAVENS. OLDER RAVENS TEND TO MOVE IN PAIRS.

WHAT MAKES THIS SUCH AN INCREDIBLY STRONG TEAM? THE KNOWLEDGE THAT SHARING, DESPITE A SMALL INITIAL SACRIFICE, CAN CREATE GREAT BENEFITS FOR EVERYONE!

WEIGHT:
up to 4.5 lb (2 kg)

LENGTH:
up to 2 ft (65 cm)

WINGSPAN:
5 ft (1.5 m)

THEY EAT everything, even acorns, not only abandoned garbage.

RATS WITH A HEART OF GOLD

SCIENTIFIC NAME: Rattus norvegicus

I'll save you!

TEAM SIZE: at least two rats

When a rat sees another in trouble, it immediately runs to the rescue. One example is when one of these large rodents falls into the water. It immediately shouts out for help, a sound that is imperceptible to our ears, and other rats quickly arrive, attracted by the screams, to pull their poor friend to safety. It also happens when a rat is caught in a trap, one of those contraptions used by humans, who don't particularly like having these animals around the house. Once again, other rats come to the rescue and cleverly start studying the mechanism that opens the trap, with the goal of pulling out the unfortunate rodent.

IT'S AN ACT OF AUTHENTIC GENEROSITY: RATS DON'T GAIN ANY PERSONAL REWARD FROM HELPING.

THEY LIVE all over the world.

FOR RATS, LOVING THY NEIGHBOR
ISN'T JUST FOR FAMILY MEMBERS—
IT'S FOR THE WHOLE COMMUNITY.

THEY EAT everything, from mollusks to cheese.

WEIGHT: about 10 oz (300 g)

LENGTH: 6–11 in (15–28 cm), plus tail, another 6 in (15 cm)

DOLPHINS WHO CARE FOR OTHERS

SCIENTIFIC NAME: Delphinidae (family)

No one gets left behind!

TEAM SIZE: from 10 up to 1,000 individuals

There are about 40 species of dolphins, and they are among the most generous animals on the planet. They form groups that help each other, cooperating for hunting as well as for protection. For example, when a dolphin is attacked by a shark, its companions immediately intervene. They hit and bite the predator so their friend has a chance to escape. If a dolphin gets stuck in some fishing nets, the others try to free it. These animals also take care of each other. Some act as midwives, helping mothers to give birth to their calves. They have also developed behavior that is unique in nature, if we exclude humans: when a dolphin is sick or injured and can no longer swim, its friends flank it on either side, holding it up by the fins to keep it from drowning.

THEY LIVE in every ocean.

THIS IS BECAUSE DOLPHINS BELIEVE THAT EVERY INDIVIDUAL IS IMPORTANT.

DOLPHINS HELP EACH OTHER IN EVERY WAY, SHOWING INCREDIBLE TEAMWORK! THAT'S NOT ALL: THEY OFTEN TRY TO SAVE THE LIVES OF OTHER SPECIES IN DANGER, SUCH AS STRUGGLING HUMANS OR WHALES CAUGHT BY FISHING VESSELS.

THEY EAT fish, mollusks, and crabs.

WEIGHT: 110-440 lbs (50-200 kg)

LENGTH: from 3 to 30 ft (1-9 m)

VORACIOUS TREE SHREWS AND PLANT "TOILETS"

I help you, you help me.

SCIENTIFIC NAME: Tupaia montana and Nepenthes rajah

TEAM SIZE: 1 tree shrew + 1 carnivorous plant

Teams aren't just for animals. For example, the mountain tree shrew has made an alliance with a plant. Here's what happens. The tree shrew, a kind of cross between a mouse and squirrel found in Asia, has a specific characteristic: when it eats, it immediately poops. It's a way to mark its territory. This "talent" is a highly useful quality for the pitcher plant, a carnivorous plant that grows in very low-nutrient soils. It compensates for this lack of nutrition by attracting the tree shrew. The plant actually has a pitcher-shaped body that is precisely the size of a tree shrew, and it garnishes its surface with sugary white pearls. The tree shrew, drawn to this tasty treat, sits over the cavity and happily starts eating.

THE REST IS EASY TO GUESS: THE TREE SHREW'S WASTE FALLS INTO THE "MOUTH" OF THE PLANT, PROVIDING NATURALLY HEALTHY NOURISHMENT.

THEY LIVE in the mountains of Borneo.

POOT!

THERE ARE COUNTLESS WAYS TO COLLABORATE AS A TEAM, THOUGH SOME METHODS ARE RATHER ... UNEXPECTED!

SIZE:
The pitcher is 16 in (40 cm) high and can hold nearly a gallon (3.5 l) of liquid.

WEIGHT:
about 7 oz (200 g)

LENGTH:
up to 16 in (40 cm)

SELFLESS FIDDLER CRAB

Hey neighbor, give me a ... claw!

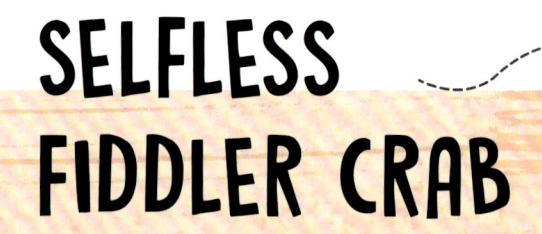

SCIENTIFIC NAME: Austruca mjoebergi

TEAM SIZE: a pair of crabs

Male fiddler crabs have a huge claw that is disproportionate to their bodies. They use it like a club to defend their home, a small hole dug into wet sand. When one crab is attacked by a larger crab trying to steal his home, he will not fight alone; his neighbor will immediately intervene to defend him. The neighbor is usually at least as big as the attacking crab, who quickly realizes he is outnumbered and is forced to flee. The alliance between the two crabs ensures that even the smallest and weakest have a safe place to call home. One might ask, "What does the big crab get out of helping his little neighbor?" Nothing, apparently. Just the added risk of losing his own home while he's helping out the smaller crab.

IN REALITY, THE BIGGER CRAB DOES ENJOY ONE ADVANTAGE: BETTER TO HAVE A WEAK, SMALL NEIGHBOR THAN A STRONG, BULLYING NEIGHBOR WHO CAUSES TROUBLE.

THEY LIVE on the northwest coast of Australia.

NEIGHBORS HELPING EACH OTHER? AUSTRALIAN FIDDLER CRABS HAVE A TEAM MENTALITY THAT IS CERTAINLY INSPIRING!

THEY EAT decaying plants and algae.

POW!

LENGTH: 10-20 mm

THE ABILITY TO COOPERATE IS THE ANSWER

As we have seen, altruism and mutual help are common, indeed very common, among many life-forms.

In some species, the ability to cooperate makes it possible for animals to organize themselves into perfectly formed swarms, herds, flocks, and packs. In others, it allows them to survive hostile environments. For some species, it has become powerful enough to create full-fledged societies, like with ants or even...

HUMAN BEINGS

who, thanks to this behavior, have gained an ecologically dominant position on Earth.

THE VERY BEST LESSON THAT CAN BE LEARNED FROM ANIMALS: COLLABORATION AND HELPING ONE ANOTHER GIVES EVERYONE AN ADVANTAGE OVER THE CHALLENGES AND DIFFICULTIES OF DAILY LIFE. AS THE OLD SAYING GOES, "UNITY IS STRENGTH!"

THERE'S STILL A LOT MORE TO DISCOVER...

If you find yourself feeling passionate about this topic and want to know more, learning the proper vocabulary will certainly help you with your research! Here are a few science terms that will help you better understand the concept of cooperation in nature.

ETHOLOGY

A **science** that studies animal behavior by observing how one species behaves compared to another. The recognized founder of this science is the Austrian zoologist **Konrad Lorenz** (1903–1989), who was awarded the Nobel Prize in 1973 for his studies of **geese**.

COMMENSALISM

This term is used when one species **benefits** from the behavior of another, without disturbing it at all—such as when **rays** follow **sharks** to eat their leftover scraps of food, a behavior that doesn't seem to make a bit of difference to the sharks. However, when **ethologists** study an example of **commensalism** more closely, they often realize that the two species are helping each other, which is **mutualism**, or that one species is actually **parasitizing** the other.

MUTUALISM

This is **altruism** among **unrelated** animals who come together just to help each other out. These animal societies are formed to ensure that, on average, everyone eats more and lives better. It can also be a way to defend their territory more effectively against enemies or predators. When this occurs between two different species, mutualism is called mutualistic symbiosis.

ALTRUISM TOWARD BLOOD RELATIVES

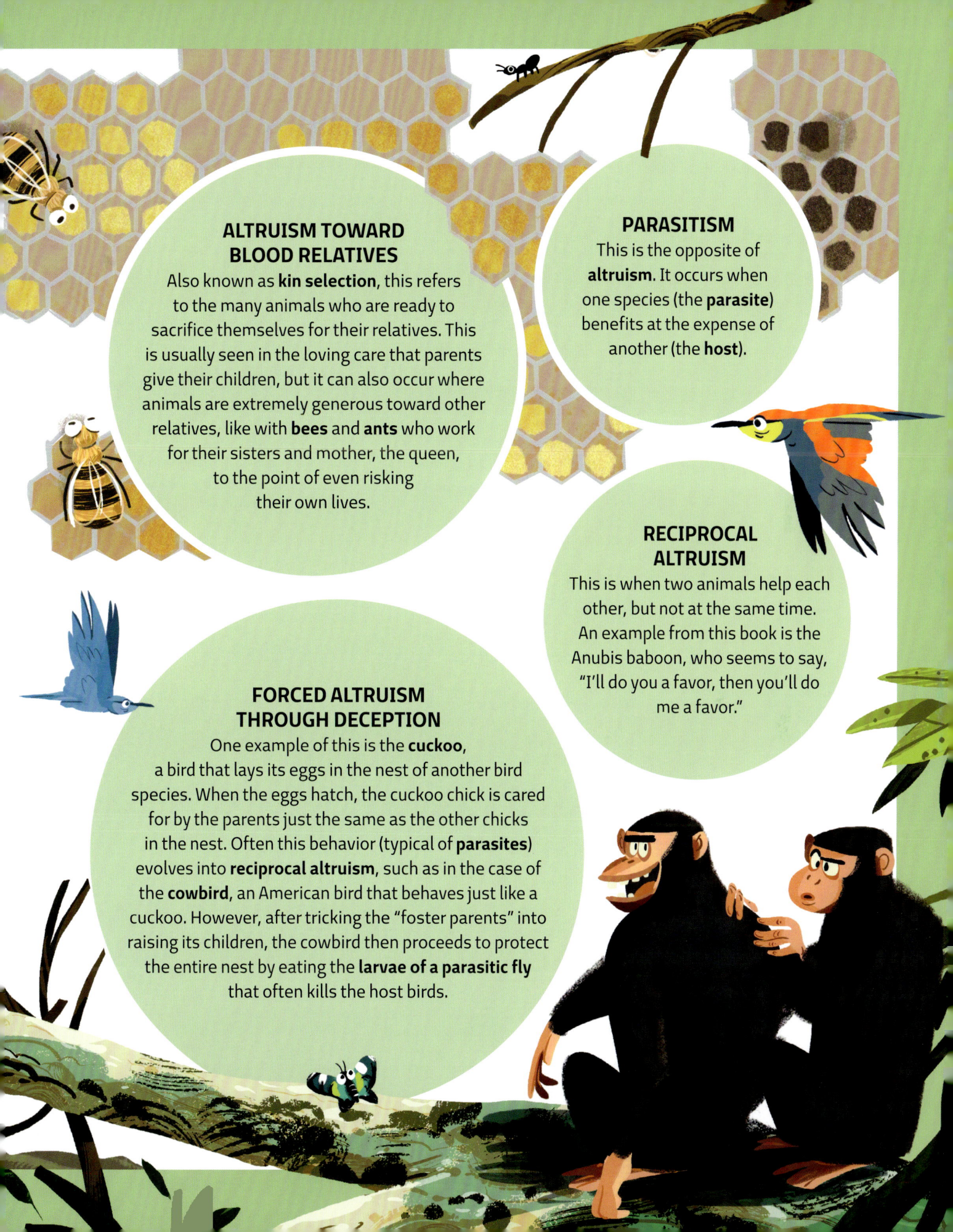

Also known as **kin selection**, this refers to the many animals who are ready to sacrifice themselves for their relatives. This is usually seen in the loving care that parents give their children, but it can also occur where animals are extremely generous toward other relatives, like with **bees** and **ants** who work for their sisters and mother, the queen, to the point of even risking their own lives.

PARASITISM

This is the opposite of **altruism**. It occurs when one species (the **parasite**) benefits at the expense of another (the **host**).

RECIPROCAL ALTRUISM

This is when two animals help each other, but not at the same time. An example from this book is the Anubis baboon, who seems to say, "I'll do you a favor, then you'll do me a favor."

FORCED ALTRUISM THROUGH DECEPTION

One example of this is the **cuckoo**, a bird that lays its eggs in the nest of another bird species. When the eggs hatch, the cuckoo chick is cared for by the parents just the same as the other chicks in the nest. Often this behavior (typical of **parasites**) evolves into **reciprocal altruism**, such as in the case of the **cowbird**, an American bird that behaves just like a cuckoo. However, after tricking the "foster parents" into raising its children, the cowbird then proceeds to protect the entire nest by eating the **larvae of a parasitic fly** that often kills the host birds.

ILLUSTRATOR
Francesco Faccia is an award-winning illustrator and comic artist. Faccia trained at the Academy of Fine Arts in Bologna where he specialized in graphic design. Francesco has since then been working in the fields of visual arts and animation. He is also winner of the Lucca Junior 2022 illustration competition.

AUTHOR
Tecnoscienza is a group of authors and educators that for more than 15 years has been involved in the dissemination of science, technology, mathematics, and the environment for numerous institutions, such as museums and companies. Their books, published in more than 20 countries, are designed to stimulate thoughts, actions, and emotions.

Graphic design and layout
Valentina Figus

WS whitestar kids™ is a trademark of White Star s.r.l.

© 2024 White Star s.r.l.
Piazzale Luigi Cadorna, 6
20123 Milan, Italy
www.whitestar.it

Translation: Qontent
Editing: Michele Suchomel-Casey

All rights reserved, including for translation, reproduction and adaptation, entirely and in part, by any means, for all countries.

ISBN 978-88-544-2098-4
1 2 3 4 5 6   28 27 26 25 24

Printed in China
by Guangzhou XY Printing Co., Ltd.

MIX
Paper from responsible sources
FSC® C178000

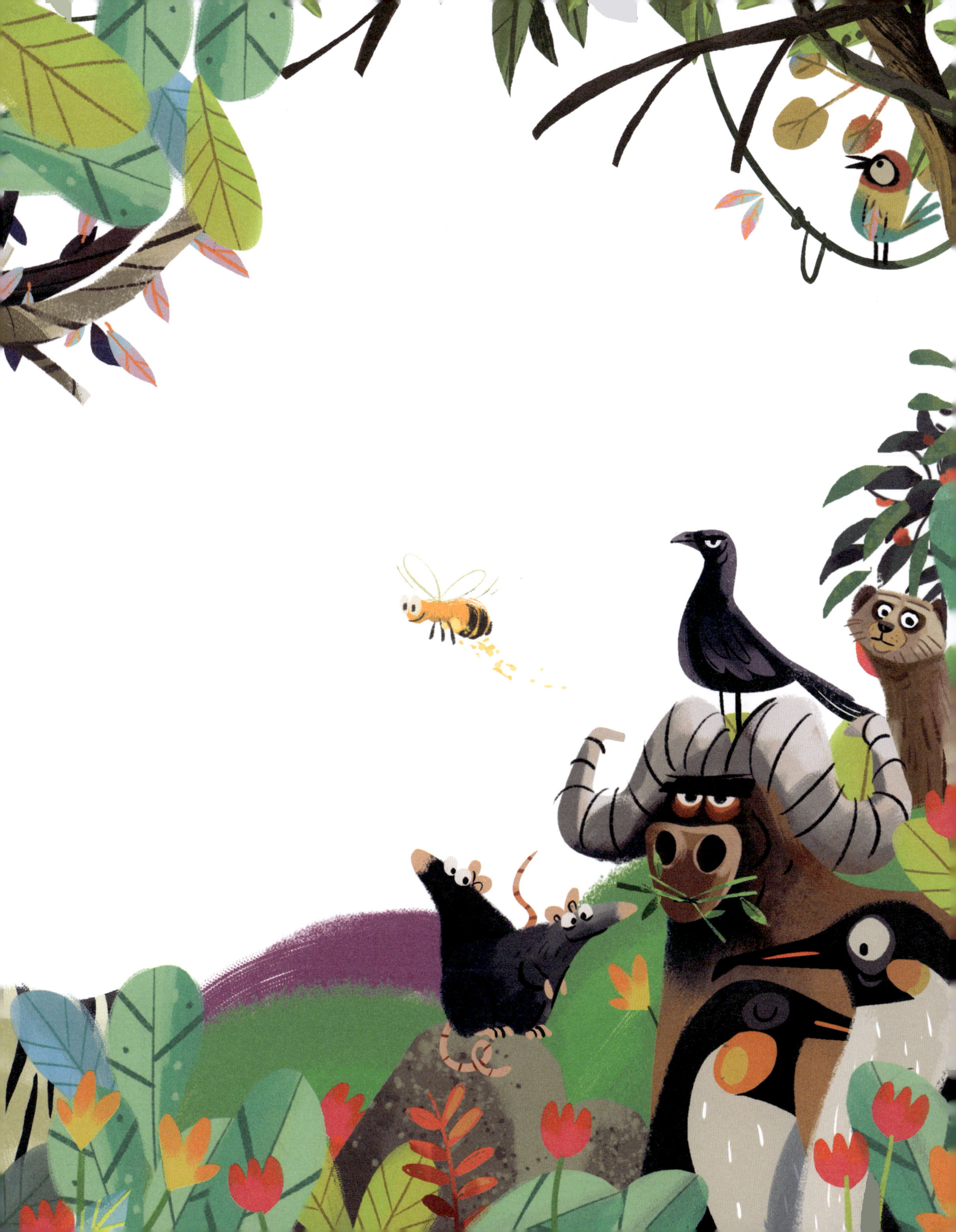